Robinhood at Shepherds Pass

Alex Mitchell

Published by Alex Mitchell, 2023.

ROBINHOOD AT SHEPHERDS PASS

First edition. October 13, 2023.

Copyright © 2023 Alex Mitchell.

ISBN: 979-8891980068

Written by Alex Mitchell.

Also by Alex Mitchell

Chapter 1

There are as many variations of the tale of Robin Hood as there have been actors who have played the role on stage and in cinema. The central premise, however, remains the same. Robin Hood was a criminal or highwayman who stole from the rich to give to the poor. A deadly game of Robin Hood would unfold in Shepherds Pass's early fall. This game would alter, test, or end the lives of those involved.

Mr. John Ashworth Sr. helped his wife empty the car of groceries. As they entered their small, modest home, Mrs. Ashworth went to close the door behind herself, and something blocked it. More accurately, someone. A man in a dark suit pushed the door open so hard that Mrs. Ashworth hit the floor. Mr. Ashworth dropped the groceries he had been carrying. A broad woman with an evil stare stood behind the man eyeing the fallen Mrs. Ashworth.

"You must be John Ashworth." The large man confirmed.

"Who are you?" Trembling, Mr. Ashworth asked.

"Well, in this case, you could say I am the Sherriff of Nottingham, and I am here to see Little John.

Another man walked in from the back room. He had broken into the rear of the house. "Kids not here."

"Well, we still have work to do." The Sheriff of Nottingham announced. "You, sir, are what's wrong with this country. You raise your children not only to show you no respect but to disrespect others and their rights and property."

Mr. Ashworth looked confused. The Sheriff of Nottingham punched him in the gut so hard Ashworth lost all his wind. He doubled over in pain. Ms. Ashworth reached out to plea with the man beating her husband, for she knew the beating had just begun. But the stocky woman slapped Mrs. Ashworth so hard she flew over a coffee table.

"These kids hack and steal everything that isn't nailed down. The government doesn't stop them. The few they catch get slaps on the wrist. Well, I came here to slap your wrist a little." The men took turns beating Mr. Ashworth as the woman beat and kicked his wife.

"Now, let's go find little John. I hope the PI is worth the money." The man representing himself as the Sheriff of Nottingham said, straightening out his tie in a broken, bloody mirror in the now ransacked home of the Ashworth's before leaving.

Chapter 2

"Code Blue. Second shift surgical team to emergency room stat. Code Blue. Surgical scrub team to emergency room stat." The automated disembodies voice called out. Then repeated it several times.

"Shit. I thought I would make it to the end of the shift without trouble." Joan Patterson, a surgeon at Shepherds Pass General Hospital, murmured more to herself than anyone in the cafeteria. She threw the half Danish she had been gnawing on in the trash and dumped her coffee and fast walked toward the emergency room. On her way, she saw Flash. Flash was the nickname for the anesthetic that was on duty. Flash was known for his 100-yard dash speed. He shot past Joan leaving a vibration in his wake. Good, she thought. I love the enthusiasm of that guy. Flash was a thin black man of medium complexion with thin-rimmed glasses who looked like he should be posing for a runner's magazine even when standing still. Joan knew she was irritable due to missing her husband. Tim Patterson is an FBI agent assigned to Shepherds Pass, and lately, they had been working shifts that had caused them to end out sleeping during different hours, if not missing each other entirely.

When Joan reached the reception desk, the first thing she noticed was that Flash was highly agitated. The reception desk was manned by Theresa, a temporary worker that had been brought in to cover regular personal, exercising earned leave.

"What's the problem, Flash? Where's our patient?" Joan asked over the repeated code blue call.

"This idiot says there is none," Flash answered.

"Watch who you call an idiot, you skinny little fool. I can bounce you off the walls." Wanda was a black woman of a much darker complexion than Flash. She wore long fake nails in an outlandish glowing shade. Wanda had false eyelashes that appeared four inches long and curled with clumps of whatever glue was used to bind them to her natural eyelashes. She was huge in a loose fat way and wore long hair extensions that did not in the slightest resemble human hair.

"What?" Joan struggled to wrap her mind around what was going on. She knew Flash to be quiet and reserved. Now here he was in full strike mode.

"Lady, shut that God Damn automated thing off." Joan finally yelled.

"Look, you doctors can't talk to people any way you want. I am a person too." Wanda defended.

"Look, lady, it's your communication system that is calling out the troops. Shut it down." Flash now seemed upset with himself for losing his cool.

Wanda reached over and turned off the switch on the panel that controlled the automated help beacon. "I never touched it. It went off by itself."

"Since you did not have an emergency, didn't it occur to you to turn it off?" Flash asked, trying to regain his composure, but Wanda's disregard was apparent, and Joan felt bad for Flash for having to acquiesce.

"Code Blue all available surgical and scrub teams to intensive care stat." The automated beacon screamed and repeated it. Flash and Joan turned and walked fast toward intensive care without a word. Before reaching the room, Flash spoke. "I am sorry, Doctor Patterson. I didn't mean to lose my cool back there. I know if a team member is seen as out of control, it reflects badly on you."

"No apology necessary, Flash. I wanted to slap the fat ass bitch myself." Joan smiled, and her candor relieved Flash. When Flash and Joan reached intensive care, it was like a staff meeting. The room was full of people wondering why they had been called there. Joan looked down at the watch and remembered it was Thursday. She had jeopardized time with her husband for whatever this malarkey was. She reached over a grabbed an aluminum bedpan. She angrily walked from the room with all eyes watching her.

"Doctor Patterson. Please don't do something stupid. I know it's not my place, but please just stop for a minute and think." Flash followed behind Joan, trying to calm her down. Joan saw a gurney with a body completely covered being wheeled from one of the rooms in her route. Joan stopped and pulled back the sheet covering the man's face. "What happened?" Joan asked the nurse wheeling the man.

"Not sure. The emergency buzzer should have gone off. He was on a drip to keep him stable. The drip stopped, but the alarm never went off. We went for a check, and he was stone-cold dead. I hate whatever is happening to the alarms around here. People are dying, and no one even wants to talk about it." The event clearly moved the nurse. Joan turned and walked even more angrily than before. She reached the IT department. "Who is in charge here?" Joan asked, and a lanky man in a bow tie raised his hand. Joan jumped on his desk and began hitting him with the bedpan. Joan is a small woman of Asian descent, and Flash knew it was his job to restrain her, but he felt uncomfortable even touching a married woman due to his strict upbringing. Flashes timidity caused the bedpan beating to persist longer than it should have. Finally, the security team was able to handcuff Joan and call the Shepherds Pass police.

Chapter 3

"Look honey the way I see it is that the work you did you did on our time, so the product you created is ours. So, hand it over." The people that had beaten the Ashworth's now sat at a table at Patrick's Bar and Grill. A middle-aged woman in a sleek business suit sat before him, and a younger woman stood behind her with her hand shoved into her purse.

"Look. The way I see it is that I gave you information to help you have arrested someone that stole from your employer or at least to reach reconciliation. Now I find that you are hospitalizing couples using the product." The woman speaking was Hellen Norcross, a private investigator. Hellen was licensed in Missouri but seldom visited Shepherds Pass.

"I aint a guy you can cross, honey." He stared coldly into her eyes.

"Half the people in this place are cops, so if you have something stupid in your mind, you had better forget it. Take your money. We don't accept blood money."

The angry mob-connected trio gave the two investigators a cold stare and then walked out, leaving the money.

"That's why I hate working for gangsters. They take everything so person." The country twang of the younger woman standing remined her mentor. The young woman was Shavon Culpepper from Lamont, Mississippi.

"Look, sweet pea, those guys pay cold hard cash, and they never care how you write up your taxes." Hellen knocked back a shot of whiskey while eyeing one of the Detectives seated at the bar. Patrick's Bar and Grill is the stopping point for off-duty police, firefighters and the hospital workers mainly. "What about that cop friend of yours that works here do you think we should give him a heads up before we pull out?

"No, Lavon is still pissed off with me. I am supposed to marry his brother, but I wish he would let bygones be bygones."

Hellen smiled at the men at the bar more as she drank a little more.

"Look, Shavon I am going to bring the car around. You know, the drill watch to be sure no one starts up their car to follow. Hellen sashayed out of the bar and around to the parking lot. She sat in the car, a late model Silver Lexus, as soon as she turned the key. The car exploded. A fire ball and flume of smoke that looked like a space shuttle take off. The windows of most of the vehicles on the lot shattered. A spray of shattered glass pelleted anyone and anything on the lot. Shavon, who stood in the doorway, was hurled backward, flipping over a table and hitting her head on the floor. Shavon shook her head to get the glass out, found her purse retrieved her gun and started to run out to the lot but was tackled by two uniformed police one man and one female.

Chapter 4

"I call this meeting of Robin Hood to order." Norton Goldberg announced. Norton was the leader of the young kids that called themselves Robin Hood. They were hackers. They were good in individually but together; they were a force to be reckoned with. The group sat in an old apartment building in the lower nine blocks of Shepherds Pass. It was a rundown neighborhood, but they owned the building through fake names. "What say you, Friar Tuck?" Chandler Rundgren, a short chubby geeky looking teen with a face full of ripe acne responded. "We have the fifty thousand from the hospital, and the one hundred fifty from the Atlantic City Central Holding company secured."

"Good report," Norton responded. "What have you to report Maid Marian?"

Carla Shields, their Maid Marian, answered. "We have a homeless center in Los Angeles that is in dire need of assistance. They are turning scores of hungry people away. Local politicians want them eradicated because they have aided the children of illegals." The group sat in a room full of expensive computer equipment, including two mini mainframes.

"They must be fed we shall send them funds." Norton proclaimed. "Is there any other business?"

"Yes." A tall thin red-headed teen held up his hand. His name was Millard Hoffland, he was known as Archer.

"Speak, Sir Archer."

"Sir Robin, there is a couple of female private investigators asking questions around town. They are searching for Little John."

"I see, and what do you recommend?" Norton asked.

"Sir, if I may be so bold." John Ashworth interrupted.

"Continue," Norton stated, and the five others in the meeting nodded.

"I recommend we arm ourselves just in case. The investigators may be no great threat, but they may lead a trail of near dwells."

"Good thinking." Joshua Franklin, a tall black teen, commented. His nickname was Harper.

"Then, if all is settled, I call this meeting to an end. Now I heard you guys downloaded the latest version of the war game. Let's order the pizza and see what it's got." Norton concluded.

"Here. Here. And no anchovies this time they give me heartburn." Maid Marian recommended.

Chapter 5

"**A**bby, why is that guy staring at us like that?" Lavon sat at his desk doing paperwork, trying to ignore the man across the room that was giving him and Abby an evil stare.

"That is Detective O' Leary. He is a friend of Lucas. He is probably trying to figure out which of us he hates the most." Lavon had been in a charity boxing match that crippled Detective Lucas.

"I didn't know you spoke Chinese?" A clerk had walked up to Lavon's desk.

"What makes you think I speak Chinese?" a greatly puzzled look overtook Lavon's face.

"Well, sir your presence is requested at the women's lockup. They have a prisoner there whose only word she can say in English is your name."

Lavon looked at Abby. "Can I come? Please. Please." Abby bounced in her chair like a little kid.

"Why not? This sounds like it is going to be perfectly humiliating, so why shouldn't someone get a laugh."

"SO, DETECTIVE, WHEN you learn speak Chinese do you still have that funny accent?" The guard leading Joan Patterson in handcuffs into the room asked.

"What accent?"

Abby laughed and slapped Lavon on the back.

"Does she have to be here?" Joan asked, eyeing Abby.

"Joan, this isn't my house. I don't make the rules here. They don't want me alone in the room with a woman prisoner without a female present." He looked at the guard. "Can you take the cuffs off her and put them on my partner."

The guard removed the cuffs and left the room.

"You beat up someone with a bedpan?" Lavon confirmed.

Abby giggled but tried to cover her mouth.

"Come on, Lavon hear me out."

Lavon shook his head as if whatever she said would make the matter worse. "Does anyone in this building know who your husband is?" Lavon asked.

"No. And you aren't going to call him. I need you to get me out of here."

Lavon stood thinking, and Abby had to ask. "Who is her husband?"

"FBI agent Tim Patterson," Joan answered.

"Wow. Country boy, I told you this would be good." Abby concluded.

"You can't tell him eighter."

"I can't keep secrets behind the back of a married man about his wife. I might burst into flames the next time I walk into a church." Lavon stated.

"Look, I am not asking you to lie for me. Just delay telling him until I can see him first."

"Why Joan?" Abby asked.

"Well, if you must know, we have been so busy we haven't." She stopped and looked embarrassed.

"Are we talking date night?" Lavon asked.

"Good way to say it. For two weeks. And it's my work that keeps getting in the way. If he finds out now, he will be too tense to." She paused again. "And we both need it, if you know what I mean."

"You want me to withhold information from your husband long enough for you to satisfy your marital urges?"

"See, I knew you would understand."

The female guard that had led Joan in returned. "Popular man today." She looked at Lavon. The got a female suspect from the bombing upstairs she says she only wants to speak to you.

"What bombing?" Lavon and Abby called out in harmony.

"Let this one go. She has diplomatic immunity." Lavon instructed the guard. What is the name of the one that wants to talk upstairs?

"Shavon Culpepper."

Lavon sank into a chair with his head in his hands. "Just when I was starting to think this day couldn't get any worse."

Detective Lopez. A female detective. Led Shavon into the room wearing an orange jumpsuit. Shavon's wrists were bound, and the chain leading to her feet was shackled.

"Well, Shavon, orange is your color," Lavon stated.

"Get me out of this shit." Tyler.

"What you got, Lopez?" Abby asked. Abby and Lopez were not friends, but they were able to work together.

"She was with the victim before the blast. Cameras inside Patrick's show her and the other woman passing a sack of cash back and forth with three unidentified mob types. This little princess has her hand on her gun the entire conversation."

"Anything to say, Shavon?" Lavon asked.

"Yeah, fuck you."

"See if you can find out which guys in the department have the biggest hands. I think it's time for a cavity search. I can get my cell phone camera." Lavon stated.

"God. I love it when you are evil." Abby stated.

"Look, Lavon you can't have a stranger reaching around inside me I am supposed to marry your brother."

"Well, after enough reaching, they won't be strangers, will they?"

"I am a licensed private investigator. Licensed in the state of Missouri."

"You know you cannot be involved in an active police investigation. And it damn well means you can't hold back information in a homicide. And by the way if they didn't teach you in Private Eye school, an exploding car with a dead body is an open police investigation." Lavon stood and stared at Shavon. "You want my help. This is me helping. Talk to the detective."

"Lady, he was your only lifeline. My suggestion to you is to apologize for that fuck you comment and hope he recovers fast, or you could lose your license. Even if we don't hold you."

"Who were you working for?" Lavon asked.

"I want a lawyer," Shavon answered.

Lavon got up and walked toward the door.

"Lavon, I am sorry. Not just about the name calling but about everything." Shavon mumbled.

Lavon did not look back as he walked through the door. Lopez caught Lavon and Abby before they could get on the elevator. "Any help you guys can give, I would appreciate. No one is going to let you work directly on a case that involves your sister-in-law."

"She aint my sister-in-law." Lavon snapped.

"Yeah, I certainly like this meaner version of you. Any idea what Wrangler Jane is doing in town." Abby asked.

"Yeah, that's what's bugging me."

Chapter 6

A maid led Lavon and Lynn into the grand dining room of Nolen Dodd. Nolen Dodd was one of Lynn's Uncles. He was a reputed crime boss, and the Dodd family had built Shepherds Pass, and its unfortunate history was inwoven into every facet of the community.

"I would like to formally apologize for the accusations I made about the relationship between you and my niece." Nolan Dodd stated the thundering boom of his voice. JoAnn, his sister, sat beside him, smiling as if the apology had been her most outstanding achievement. "I accept your apology, and I truly hope we can move past in misguided ill that may exist between us." Lynn seemed shocked at Lavon's well thought out acceptance of the apology. She knew he must have been thinking about the possibility that the air needed to be cleared between the two men. She was also not clear what the conversation was since she and Lavon limited conversation on open investigation. During the dinner, most of the small talk was made by JoAnn. She approved of Lynns relationship with Lavon.

After dinner, Nolan asked Lavon to join him in his den for a smoke and a glass of brandy. It was clear Lynn did not like the move. She felt she was being discriminated against for being a woman but chose not to protest even though Lavon knew she was unhappy about the gesture.

Nolen handed Lavon a glass of brandy. "You have been an athlete. You probably don't drink much. It always amazes me that liquor endorsements are almost exclusively by pro athletes, and the ones I know drink very little."

Lavon accepted the glass and sipped. He found the drink was much better than he expected. There was no acidity, and the flavor was smooth and well-aged. "I don't drink much, but this is probably the best brandy I have ever had."

"A family I know. The Pettibone's make it. They have for years."

"Did we come here to discuss fine liquor?" Lavon asked.

"No. We came here to discuss how easy it can be to make a mistake in judgment."

"You apologized for misjudging me. I accepted."

"Certainly. But it is a future misjudgment that I am concerned about. You may misjudge me."

Lavon was confused.

"Are you working on that car bombing thing?"

"Not directly, but any detective that can assist when needed. Is there something I should know?"

"Yes. That upsets me. And I had nothing to do with it."

The picture Lavon had in front of him now became more in focus. "You are saying that it is gangland style, but it was not something that had anything to do with you?"

"I am saying do what you do. Find out what happen, and if you kill someone in the process, it won't hurt my feeling in the least." With this last statement, Nolen had left the room. He had abandoned the conversation for the evening and there was no recalling it.

"SO, WHAT DID YOU BIG strong men have to discuss that did not involve us, poor frail women?" Lynn asked after she and Lavon had returned to her mansion. There had been no conversation on the dive home. Lavon was lost in his thoughts. The day had presented so much to ponder. Lynn was a little angry about being left out of the talk. Whatever it was. But angrier that Lavon did not seem to notice she was upset. Lynn walked to the bedroom door and stood in front of it. "Don't think for a minute you are going to slither out of here before we have our real first fight, and this is your home."

"Turn around." Lavon requested, and Lynn turned with her back to him. He released the catch on the necklace she wore. He placed the chain on the dresser. "My uncle has no right to auction me off if that was the discussion. You would have to talk to me directly. In case you have not realized, it's a whole new world. They even let women vote."

Lavon began unbuttoning her dress. "He wanted to tell me he had nothing to do with an open case." Lavon proceeded to unbutton the buttons. He kissed the back of her neck.

"Mr. Tyler, you clearly have no understand of how a first fight is supposed to work."

Lavon helped the dress from her shoulders, and it fell to the floor. He unclasped her bra and removed it. Still, she stood, not facing him. He began massaging her shoulders.

"Lynn, I love you. Not just the physical side of you. But also, the friendship part of you and the intellectual side of you that helps me with thoughts that get bogged down." He pressed against her, and she could hear his heartbeat. "If you want to fight. Then fight. I was talking to a friend today about wasting quality time and not being able to make that time up and how crazy it makes us." Lynn turned around. "Well, maybe we can just skip to the makeup sex part." She whispered. And they did.

Chapter 7

Lavon and Abby sat at the bar at Patrick's. The place had not yet been reopened to the public, but there were still a herd of police, fire department, and insurance people milling about, so the staff at Patrick's had provide coffee and donuts. Lavon explained to Abby his conversation with Nolan. "Do you think he wants you to hit someone that is encroaching on his turf?" Abby asked.

"I think he is saying if I run into these guys, they are dangerous and desperate, and they don't belong to him."

"Well, since your brother's girl is in the middle it would be wise to stay clear anyway."

Lavon could see Tim Patterson walking up. He had asked him to meet him and Abby at Patrick's.

"You and my wife got a thing going on you want to maybe talk about?" Were the first words out of Patterson's mouth?

'Relax, J. Edgar, I was in the room. She only asked him to postpone telling you until she had a chance to jump your bones." Abby corrected. "How did that turn out?"

Tim looked almost embarrassed at Abby's forwardness. "So, what did you two need?"

"I hear you got a couple or tech geniuses over at the fed. First, I wonder if they can put together a presentation to tell us what we are looking for so we don't destroy evidence should we lumber across some in the way of hacking stuff. And second, could you have someone look at the hospital where your wife works and see what they can tell us about the level of computer threat."

"You mean because you have a dead body there, and you don't want some smart kid knocking off grandma for the family jewels by remote shutting down her heart monitor?" Patterson picked up a donut and began devouring it. "Who do you think blew up the Lexus?"

"My brother, Lovester's girlfriend, was one of the intended victims. And she won't talk to me if I won't help get her out."

"So why don't you try to get her out?"

"Because he can feel she is holding back, and so can I and I just met Annie Oakley."

LAVON AND ABBY HAD just returned to the department and noticed Officer Webber waiting. Webber is a female officer with short, cropped hair and a solid athletic build. She is married to one of the women who works for the fire department. As Abby approached Webber, they stared at each other. The two women had come close to a confrontation in the past.

"Alright, knock it off, both of you. This is a place of work." Lavon broke the staring contest.

"I got something I need to ask you?" Webber stated, and Abby turned to give them some privacy. "No, both of you."

"Sure, what you got?"

"Well, the other night I went on a call, and I think the detective got it wrong. No offense to him, but I think he was tired, and it was getting near the end of his shift." Webber began explaining.

"So, based on your years as a glorified crossing guard."

"Stop that shit, Abby. She is trying to be professional." Lavon interjected.

Webber laid a bunch of photos on the desk and spread them out. "The call came in, and from the neighbors said the two may have been beating up on each other. We get there, and both the man and wife are passed out on the floor. The whole house is busted to pieces. Both have bruises galore."

"So, it happens cross complaint cancels each other out in some spousal abuse cases."

"No victim, no crime." Abby stated.

"Yeah, that's the way it was written up but take a look at this guy's bruises with his shirt off from the hospital photo."

In an instant Lavon saw with was bothering Webber.

"See, I have been in Shepherd a long time and I know this is a small town. It aint common for a lot of big things to happen at the same time. I think this is part of a bigger puzzle. Now Lavon, I know you put puzzles together. Do you see what I see?" Webber seemed embarrassed to have referred to Lavon by his first name before Abby but quickly decided to let it go.

Lavon smiled at Webber. It took an instant longer, and Abby saw what was wrong in the photos.

"What is the wife's ring finger size?" Abby asked.

"About a six, I would say," Webber answered, looking directly at Abby.

"And that is a thumbprint and for finger where someone lifted this guy off the ground the flung him. Someone with a pair of hands three times the size of mine." Lavon assessed.

"So, I think we should ask the wife if she grows a big strong pair of hands when she is provoked." Abby joked.

"That would be a first." Webber stated and started to collect the picture leaving the address.

"Good catch, patrolman." Lavon assessed.

"Damn good catch." Abby seconded, and this brought a slight smile to Webber.

"So, what are you thinking?" Abby asked as Webber left.

"I think there is a certain bunch of people that know how-to beat-up people badly without killing them. Loan sharks, mob collectors, you know the type that can beat up a person once a week and make them hurt bad but never kills them because then they don't stand a chance of collecting."

"So, Mr. and Mrs. Normal got a visit from the ass-kicking fairly; why?"

"We will have to ask them that, but you remember Nolan told me there were gangsters in town he had no control over. I wonder if they hire hillbilly girl private detectives."

Chapter 8

"I call this meeting of our merry little band together with a heavy heart. It has been brought to my attention that barbarians have attacked the home of Little John and have brought pain and embarrassment to his family. How do you say we respond." Norton, in his best Robin Hood persona stated.

"Sir, I Sir Archer, say we are lucky to find a foe willing to combat us and we should take the challenge as an opportunity to show our prowlessness in battle."

"Do tell."

"So far, we operate at the barest minimum of our capacity both in machinery and intellectual powers. In front of us is a foe that still thinks in terms of physical might."

"I, Friar Tuck agree we all knew that one day we may need to leave Shepherds Pass. The question is do we leave as dogs with our tails between our legs or do we leave with our heads held high."

"Does anyone disagree?" Norton asked and there was silence. "Good so be it. Friar strip Atlantic Central Banking of every dime if you can. Raid as many of the companies as you can and build a parting bounty. Put traveling money in the offshore accounts then send donations to the list of one hundred neediest charities we have compiled."

"Sir, I Maid Marian ask what of the police and the private investigators that hunt us?"

"Those that delight in the hunt should rejoice in the chase. I Sir Harper say lets us set off fire department alarms and shut down traffic lights all over town. Let them spend energy chasing shadows and leading the blind to light."

"Well stated there is much work to do."

The group went to work hacking into companies bouncing the traces off overseas servers, so it looked like the hacking was coming from outside the US. A portion of the group spent time filling the bank account of charities using fictitious names. They hacked into the 911 system and called out fire alarms to various locations. They also maxed out the credit card of Shavon Culpepper and reported her car rental as a stolen car. "Thou this may not be enough. I say it is time for a direct confrontation." Proclaimed Maid Marian.

Chapter 9

Shavon drug her rolling suitcase to the lobby of the motel where she had been staying. She noticed through a window that the rental car she had acquired was being looked at by local police officer. Good riddance to this town she thought. She had been advised by her lawyer to check out of Shepherds Pass and let him handle the confrontation with the police. She had spoken by phone to S. Rowen Tyler; Lavon's father seeking help and was scolded instead. There was an elderly couple in front of her checking out and she noticed there was a tall think kid in a hoodie standing staring at her. Before she could think why the kid looked so familiar, he pulled out a gun and pointed it at her. Shavon ducked and clutched her purse only to remember the Shepherds Pass police had not returned her gun. The first bullet went past her and shot an excellence award off the top of the motel counter. Shavon was now on the move running toward the side entrance to the motel. There were two more shots. Then something stung like being stuck in the butt by a hot branding iron. He shot me in the ass she thought falling forward and sliding through the automatic doors. One of the heels of her shoes had come off. As she was stumbling to stand and continue her run a girl in a green hoodie stood over her and pointed a gun at her. "I Maid Marian say die at my hand witch. I claim your life as mine." Shavon saw the revolver and heard the hammer click. Then there was a loud gunshot followed by two more. Shavon opened her eyes not knowing she had closed them and the girl in the green hoodie lye there with a huge blood stain in the middle of her chest. What was happening Shavon thought as the broad woman from the meeting with Hellen ran and jumped over her in pursuit of the teen that had chased her into the aim of Maid Marian. There was a barrage of gunfire coming from the front parking lot. Gee Lavon, I fucked you around again, she thought to herself.

Lavon and Abby noticed the home of the Ashworth couple was still a shambles when they arrived. Lavon and Abby had spent the past few hours in the meeting with the FBI cyber threat specialist having their skill level updated. The Ashworth couple looked totally defeated. Their resolve had been drained to a point where they had lost interest in cleaning up the mess from the disaster that had caused them such grief.

"Mr. Ashworth who did this to you and your wife?" Abby asked. She Lavon sat on a ragged sofa across from Ashworth's.

"No one we did this ourselves." Mrs. Ashworth lied.

"No ma'am you did not. But before you plan on lying to me again, please let me explain something to you and your husband. The people that do what they did to you are pros. They beat people to within an inch of their lives. Then they come back again and again until they get what they want. Soon all your hope is gone. You are more than physically beat up. Mentally you are far worse injured."

"There were three of them. Two men and a woman. The big man said he was the Sheriff of Nottingham, and he was here for Little John." Mr. Ashworth answered clutching his wife.

"Sir you have a son. A junior, is that right?" Abby screamed.

"Yes, they said they wanted to teach us a lesson on parenting." Mrs. Ashworth commented.

"We need you to make a list of his friends. If you have pictures of them, find them and we will need to see his room." Abby shouted. Lavon knew something that had been said triggered something in Abby and now it was time to let it flow through her.

"What is it, Abby?" Lavon asked when the Ashworth's retrieving the required items.

"It's Rood Hood and his merry men."

"That an old myth."

"No dick wad it's a video game and with got a bunch of genus level teen playing it against a bunch of stone-cold gangsters in real life on the streets. Sad thing is I am not sure who to root for."

Lavon and Abby sat with Detective Lopez in the office that was now Lt. Don Nash's. Nash had been promoted to Lieutenant recently with Lieutenant Dana Crawford had been promoted.

"What do we have?" Don started.

"Well officially Lavon is not on the case, but we would not have anything much if it had not been for him and Detective Blackwell." Lavon noticed how Lopez seemed more eager to make up with Abby than Abby was ready to accept it. "The three people from the car bombing are Lowell Kaiser, Sherman Frakes and Gesell Finch career bad assess. They work for Atlantic City notable Donovan Malone."

"Why?" Nash's first question was expected.

"Hacking and computer theft. A group of kid geniuses decided to steal money from rich gangsters, and we believe they have been donating the money to charity or causes. It's based on Robin Hood." Abby entered.

"That's crazy." Nash commented.

"Very. They have been tracking the theft for a while. We assume and need some private investigator with connection and license to operate in Shepherds Pass." Lavon pointed out.

"That is where Hellen and your future sister-in-law come in?"

"We believe the private investigators lead them to the home of Mr. and Mrs. Ashworth where the couple received a severe beating." Abby explained.

"Someone was shooting at your sister-in-law at a local motel. We have her in custody just in case in the General Hospital. The witnesses say they saw kids start the gun play. What the hell does that have to do with Robin Hood?" Nash asked.

"It's Robin Hood the video game not the legend precisely." Abby explained.

"Kids who don't know where fantasy end and reality begin. Now we have a dead teenage girl and a uniformed cop the took two non-fatal rounds. What is next in this tale?" Nash asked.

"Well Elroy Hadley, the cyber-crimes specialist that conducted the lecture this morning wants to meet us at the hospital. He says he has information for us." Lopez announced.

"If Lopez doesn't mind. There is a uniform cop named Webber who worked at high school community involvement programs. If she isn't too busy, why do we have her clarify who the rest of the merry men are. She can speak to the teens on their level or otherwise we might end up with a list of nick names to decode." Lavon listened to the suggestion of Abby, and it was perfect. Lavon and Abby had recently had a clash of wills because of her drinking problem, and she was working to fix it. This sounded to him like she was clearly on the road to recovery.

"Sounds like a plan. For some reason fire alarms keep going off and there is no fire. Then the traffic lights are going down for no reason. But I will find a way to get Webber on point.

Chapter 10

Lavon and Abby walked into the hospital room of Shavon. There had been a uniformed policeman guarding the door. Shavon lay face down handcuffed to the bed. She wore a robe that opened in the back and was covered with a towel to cover her naked butt. Lavon walked in and lifted the towel. "Yeah, it's Shavon alright I would recognize those cheeks anywhere."

"Hey lady cop isn't that some form of sexual harassment or something?" Shavon uttered.

"Not unless he insults it. And by the way it really is nice, but you may have to consider a tattoo to cover the extra whole."

"I hate you Lavon this is all your fault. I called your daddy, and he says you can't have people reaching inside me."

"So, what is it with the two of you?" Abby asked. Abby had recently lectured Lavon about partners need to tell each other everything important.

"Well, if mister perfect didn't tell you maybe I should. There as a bridal shower and we hired male strippers. His finance screwed one guy in the middle of the floor in front of all of us."

Abby looked at Lavon shocked. She now knew the cross he bared, and she was not sure it was meant for her to know. She wondered how the hell this guy was keeping it together.

"Well, that is just like you Shavon. Telling everybody else's dark dirty secrets but leaving out your own."

"What's that supposed to mean." Shavon tried her best to play innocent.

"I know what you did at the party too. I always have. I know you started the ball rolling you might say. And with the strippers and one of them was a girl as I understand it. To this point I have tried to spare my brother from hearing what a whore you can be but not now." Lavon was beyond furious.

"Oh, God Lavon please don't tell Lovester. When he gets home from over there, I want a storybook wedding. I want to be a Tyler girl." Shavon was now crying and trying to hide her face.

"Two days ago, you could have told us that you were working for the enforcers of Donovan Malone. A teenage girl would still be alive. Helen might still be alive. We got people dying on our watch and the only thing you seem to be worried about again is covering you own ass. No more." Lavon removed the towel covering her butt and threw it on the floor to make his point. "Twenty-four hours you tell my brother, or I will. You give Detective Lopez anything she need to track down these bastards or I turn what we have to Patterson at the FBI, and they will pull all your licenses and permits. And Shavon, you can cry enough tears to bring back the dead." Lavon looked Abby. "Partner, I think we got a meeting upstairs to get to."

Lavon usually wore a sports jacket and jeans. Before they entered the meeting with the FBI and the hospital personal Abby grabbed the back of his jacket. "Hey farm boy I got to ask you two questions."

"Shoot."

"Are you sure your head is on straight?"

"Yeah, I am still mad as hell at her but."

"But nothing. You should be mad. There are girls and guys out there that won't be happy until they turn the person that is special to you into the tramp they are. If you love your brother, you can't let him marry that tramp, it will poison your relationship with him when he finds out you knew about her before he married her. Second question. Does Lynn know?"

"She knows but not the details."

"In this case the detail makes the meal. Don't let her find out in anybody else's words but your own."

"Why are you trying to help me, Abby."

"Turnabout, nine out of ten days you cover me. This must be the tenth day. Beside I don't know if we are friends or just partners but manipulating women make it hard or the rest of us."

"Still feels good having you rescue me for a change."

"Shut up plow boy we got work to do."

Lavon and Abby entered the meeting room and sat. Joan Patterson had been asked by Agent Hadley to attend. Joan was eyes nervously by Bert Covington the head of the IT department and the man that Joan had bashed with the bed pan.

"Usually in this type of meeting I like to start by saying I have some good news and some bad news. I could say it but that would be lying." Hadley began.

"How bad is the bad news?" Detective Lopez asked. She had been anxious for the meeting to begin. Lopez had notice Hadley's face and knew he had found something important.

"Well for starters there is a Trojan hidden in the computer programs that run the monitoring equipment."

"Wait how could there be?" Covington seemed shocked.

"Simple someone walks in the front door. They probably complain about a headache or heavy menstrual cycle. They make note of the type of computers you have. The number of workstations with computers that are not locked when not in use. And then they report to a second person that lays out a plan to infect your system. Once inside your system the virus is spread to your primary business functions."

"Wait you are saying the man that died because his drip would not come on and the alarm wound not sound was because some smart ass planted a virus to get records?" Joan seemed angry.

"Why don't we let Mr. Covington answer that one. How much money did you give then the first time?" Hadley's question took everyone at the table by storm. "And before you answer remember lying to the FBI is a crime."

"Fifty thousand."

"What?" Joan screamed.

"Look they locked up operations until I agreed to pay a ransom." Covington confessed.

"How much the second time?"

"Another fifty, but it was not my idea to pay. The insurance company paid the second and third times." Everyone was staring at Covington. "You don't understand they got into record. They stole all the social security numbers, credit card numbers, passwords, you name it." Covington was now sweating and looking sorry for himself.

"Lavon and Abby when you searched John junior's room those boxes you were worried about. You were correct to be worried." Hadley acknowledged.

'What boxes?" Joan asked.

"Empty system software boxes for two different mini main frame computers." Lopez answered.

"By giving them the money, they asked for they now have a better computer system running than the hospital and the police department." Hadley explained.

"She only hit you with a bed pan." Abby mocked.

"Well, with dead bodies, car explosions and a renegade computer system I think it might be time to contact the NSA. This is getting into their ball court now that they have the capacity of major terrorist." Hadley noted.

"So far, it's been all about the game. Rood Hood." Abby reminded.

Chapter 11

Gesell stepped onto the second-floor walkway outside her motel room. She thought it a major inconvenience that the motels don't allow smoking in the rooms. Sherman walked to her from his next-door room and held out a light to light her cigarette. Sherman and Lowell had been sharing a room next door to Gesell. Now Lowell was in the room giving a progress report to Malone, their boss, and it was not going well. Lowell needed cigarettes as much as Gesell. As the flame reached the tip of Gesell's cigarette it bent slightly as the whisp of a slight breeze changed the direction of the air. Sherman looked at Gesell and her eyes showed frozen surprise. There was also now an arrow sticking out of her throat. "A gift from Maid Marian." Sherman heard a young man's voice yell out. There were two old woman that were housekeepers loading their carts to clear rooms. Now they saw Gesell with the arrow sticking out of her neck and descending to the floor. They also saw Sherman pull his gun. The housekeepers started screaming hysterically. "Shut up. You, old bags. I can't tell where the arrow came from with all that racket." Sherman yelled at them. Lowell stuck his head out the door with the phone still in one hand and his gun in the other. "New development Boss." Lowell mumbled into the phone.

Abby, Lopez, and Lavon met Webber and Wendell at the motel where Gesell had been wasted. "She checked in with the two men. They had the next-door room, but they hightailed it out of here. They match the description of the Atlantic City thugs you are looking for?" Wendell reported. Wendell was a uniformed cop that had recently been promoted to Sargent. He is a good friend of Lavon's. "Any chance they went back to New Jersey?"

"What is a word for less than none?" Abby answered.

"I got your list of kids. They are a tight group." Webber reported handing the list of names and alias to Lopez. "They were put out of the local junior college for illegal use of the campus computers. They all reported to their families that they are away at college. They send bogus mail redirected from someone living in the city where they say are in school."

"Archer really." Lopez exclaimed reading the list of nicknames attached to the teens.

'Well at least that explains the arrow." Lavon surmised.

"Good work Webber." Abby commented and the surprise showed on Wendell's face. Wendell and Webber have always been good friends so when Wendell and Abby had a falling out Webber and Abby also were swept into the tide of ill feelings.

"Well, I got dinner at the mayor's house tonight. Anybody want to guess what I won't be discussing?" Lavon's comment caused the group to laugh.

"So, the two of you go visit that Gangster Nolan before you come to see me. Should I be offended?" Mayor Carlton Dodd another of Lynn's uncles asked as Lynn and Lavon joined him and Sean Hardcastle, the Mayors public relations manager.

"We accepted invitations in the order received. Please save your jealousy for more appropriate occasions." Lynn smartly answered digging into her meal. After much silence Sean asked. "So, Lavon how is the car bombing thing coming?"

"Not sure it's not my case Lopez caught it. She is capable." Lavon's smiled and kept eating.

"I would have thought Nash would have put you on it right away. Maybe I should give him a call. What are you working on that is so important?"

"Helping get cats down from trees." Lavon answered and Lynn laughed and kicked him under the table.

"The truth is my brother Lovester is engaged to one of the people involved in the bombing thing and it would be unethical for me to get too close to that case. We wouldn't want the FBI to think we were running a crooked shop."

"What about the teenage girl that was shot in the motel lobby?"

"More cats, more trees. That one is not my case eighter. Or the one you probably haven't heard about where the woman was shot in the neck with an arrow."

The mayor continued to eat watching Sean's bad attempt to pump information from Lavon.

"Maybe someone should light a fire under Nash. You are a waisted resource." Sean offered a backhanded compliment.

"Did you and Dolan discuss anything important?" The mayor finally showed what was on his mind.

"Yes. Very." Lavon answered, accepting dessert.

"Well." the mayor prompted.

"Well, we both think that it is a shame and misleading that so many athletes advertise alcohol when a lot of them drink very little if at all." Lynn chucked and tried to hide it with a napkin then kicked Lavon again.

"Lavon, had you ever thought about a career in politics? A former college football star. From a large Christian family. Father is a noted novelist and former Police Chief. A former Marine and current Detective. I think there are plenty of people that would rally behind you." The mayor noted.

"That would be if you don't align yourself the wrong side of the Dodd history." Sean mentioned coldly.

"WELL, THAT WAS COMICAL if not a little embarrassing." Lynn noted when she and Lavon were alone at home.

"You mean the Gangsters apologize for bad manners. Then we have dinner with the mayor, and he throws a bribe on the table."

Lynn cornered Lavon and began unbuttoning his shirt. "Now you see why I have spent my entire adult life try to clean up the mess created by my own blood." Lynn began removing Lavon's shirt and he stopped her. "It's time I tell you the whole story about why I left Casey, my ex-girlfriend."

"You don't have to."

"I know but it makes me feel like I am keeping secrets from you if I don't."

After the total of the tale had been laid out for Lynn the two lye intertwined. "You know you can't hate Shavon for what she did. She may have started the game of dirty dare to go further but Casey is a grown woman, and she chose to suspend her moral beliefs and wreck your relationship in the process."

'Baby I know that, but it still hurt like hell."

They lay there a little bit longer then Lynn asked. "Which one was Lovester?' She had met much of his family at a charity get together.

"You haven't met him he wasn't at the get together."

"That impossible I thought everybody was there and I do mean everybody."

"No, he is deployed in the middle east."

"Wow there are a lot of you guys. Are you going to really tell him?"

"I have a feeling she will."

"I feel sorrier for him than you and I never met the guy."

Chapter 12

Little John could not make out the full backyard of his parent's neighbors, so he crept slowly. One of the neighbors' dogs began to bark but there was nothing he could do to stop it. John knew once he had the merry band hand left town the enemy would come for their parents. He wanted to give money to his parents so they would have the option to leave. John heard the snap of a branch or twig then nothing. It took a moment for him to realize perhaps it was in imagination. Little John reached for the back door and a large hand grabbed his hand. "Little John I would presume." John turned to try to run, and another large man grabbed him. They lifted John off his feet and carried him silently away into the cool Shepherds Pass night.

"Do me a favor and resist as much as you can kid, I really want to enjoy every minute of beating the snot out of you." Lowell grunted.

John was bound to a chair. Bleeding from being roughed up before thrown into a car trunk and driven wherever he was now.

"Do your worst oh sheriff of Nottingham for tonight it is me in this chair but tomorrow it will be you and your bosses will not be so polite."

"Look geek speak English. This Robin Hood Merry bullshit is giving me a headache."

"I think this little shit is warning us that whatever they planned it is too late for us to stop it." Sherman translated.

"Oh God what now? You pricks killed Gesell."

"Any you killed Marian; on that part we are even. Now you may wish to verify it with the news but tonight we donated one hundred million dollars to the Shepherds Pass Hospital. Where do you think that money came from?"

Lowell drew back to hit John but stopped and stared instead. "That is why I never had kids. You can't talk to them. Do you realize that if I try to go back to Jersey, I'm a dead man?" Lowell asked.

"Yes, you have lost in the worst possible way. But there is a way out of the forest for you if you choose."

"Great more medieval riddles," Lowell commented.

"You form a temporary alliance with Robin, and he will put millions in your account anywhere you want. New names and property." John outlined. It was now clear the merry men had planned the meeting.

"What are you asking? Kill Malone?" Sherman asked.

"No, cutting off his head would only make more snakes grow. Cut off the head of Shavon Culpepper as a show of good faith and the end to a vigorous game."

"Done."

Chapter 13

"Lavon, are you a Christian man?" Lavon sat at his desk with Abby, Lopez, and Webber around him, trying to decide the next move on the Robin Hood case. Shavon had called him on his cell phone, and her voice was irritated and irritating.

"Yes, Shavon," Lavon answered, and a choir of rolled eyeballs was set off.

"When I was shot in that motel, the housekeeping collected my luggage and locked it up. The motel says my credit cards have all been canceled or reported stolen."

"Sad."

"They took the car rental for nonpayment and said there is a stolen notice on it, so I have no way of driving out of town."

"Sadder still."

"The ambulance guys cut the clothes I was wearing into paper dolls. I called your brother, and the wedding is off, and he froze our joint bank accounts."

"I see."

"No, you don't see. I am broke, naked, hungry with a big piece of my ass missing, and hundreds of miles from civilization. These hospital people think I caused this disaster, and they want me out."

"I'll help you, Shavon." Lavon held down the phone so she could not hear him laughing. "You must agree in writing to appear in any court case we ask you to regarding the Robin Hood mess."

"Deal. And I will promise to stop being such a pain in the ass. How soon can you come?"

"Well, there is the problem. See I have a meeting here, but what I can do is send a friend of mine by. She will have clothes. A train ticket back to Lamont and some pocket money as a loan."

"Oh God, you are an angel. You know if I had not picked your brother, I might have picked you."

"Well, I surely recognize that shifty look Detective Tyler," Abby noted as he disconnected the line.

"Webber, you up for a mission?"

Chapter 14

Webber arrived at Shavon's hospital room carrying a big bag and a form to sign stating she would return for court dates if required. Shavon inspected the bag. "Oh, you have got to be kidding me." Shavon pulled out a pair of women's sweatpants that were at least four sizes too large for her, and the drawstring had been removed. "God damn you, Tyler men never forgive a woman." Webber fought back laughter to the point she had to wipe her eyes from the tears that were forming. Shavon then removed a ragged pair of oversized women's underpants. "Okay, what the hell is this supposed to be."

"I think they are called bloomers ma'am," Webber answered.

"Just the thing if I decide to screw some guy from the early 1800's." There were no socks but two tennis shoes. One was a lady's size five and the other a men's size 12. "I guess my train ticket has me riding with the baggage." The last item was a women's halter top that said honk if you love Jesus over the right breast. "Look you are a woman too how could you let him do this to me." Webber watched Shavon dress in the ridiculous outfit as best she could. Shavon had to remove the shoelace from the men's show to make a belt to hold up the baggy sweatpants.

"I may not know Lavon." She paused. "Detective Tyler very well but he doesn't strike me as the type to start an altercation. I think he is just trying to get it out of his system."

"Sure, you would take his side. Are you sleeping with him?"

"No. I am married, and I would never cheat on my spouse. Now your train ticket is real, and the ride to the station is also. Now I am going to get you something to eat it. It might take a while for the next train in your direction."

After Webber had been gone for a few minutes, Shavon decided to see if she could walk in the off-matching shoes. She was practicing walking and looking up directly into the eyes of Sherman Frakes. "Oh Shit." Shavon tried to run but the shoes did not completely cooperate.

She found herself tripping over a wheelchair that had been left in the corridors. She hit the floor face down, tried to jump and run but the shoelace she was using as a belt snapped and her pants fell to her knees, and she tripped. Smack, she felt a red-hot sting to her right butt cheek. "Oh god, not the other one." She cried out and she turned a corner and hobbled down the hall with one shoe, trying desperately not to lose her pants. She noticed a fire alarm and smacked it to set it off; the alarm went off, and blood from her hand covered the wall. She ran into the stairwell she, tripped, trying to run upstairs, and smacked face-first into the landing. She could feel Sherman behind her, he pointed his gun and would have killed her had he not stopped the split second to admire the view. The door opened at the top of the landing and there was Webber with her gun in hand. Sherman and Webber fired at the exact same time. Shermans bullet hit the right shoulder of Webber. Webbers bullet hit Sherman in the center of the forehead. Before Webber could say anything, people ran in a charge down the stairs almost trampling Webber and Shavon responding to the fire alarm.

"WHERE IS CALAMITY JANE now?" Abby asked as She and Lavon met Wendell in the hallway with Webber. Webber had been prepped for surgery to remove the bullet. "I think Joan Patterson is upstairs digging the second bullet out of her ass. Hopefully, this time without anesthesia.

"Come here." Webber commended Lavon. He walked closer to the gurney, not knowing what to expect. She gave him a one-armed hug with her free arm.

"What's that for?"

"Because you deserve it. You are far too nice to shitty people. And you blame yourself when they abuse you."

"Alright doll face let's get you in and get some drugs in you." Flash, a young anesthetist, remarked as he led a couple of nurses to assist Webber.

"Hey, Webber." Wendell called as they were wheeling her off.

"Yeah, me too. Aint it a kick in the head." Webber responded.

It took quite some time and effort for the police to calm everyone down at Shepherd Pass General Hospital. The fire department had received so many false alarms that they were stretched across the entire countryside. The malfunctioning light caused traffic jams and accidents, and if the fire had been real, the hospital would have burned to the ground.

Chapter 15

"I got a call for you on the cold line." A clerk stated as Lavon prepared to leave the squad room for the day. In a police station, the police have the right to tap all phones on the premises. In Shepherd Pass there is one phone that is never tapped or recorded; it is used for special purposes. "The caller says he is Robin Hood, and he wants to make a deal to give you the Sheriff of Nottingham. Does that make sense, or did I get the message wrong?"

"The little bastards want us to play the game?" Abby announced.

"Did anybody ever tell you that you are much too cute for a real cop. You look more like one of those tv cops." Shavon complimented Wendell as he tried to keep her on track and get her statement. Wendell was familiar with women trying to flirt with him to get out of an arrest or a ticket. Her charms did not affect him whatsoever. Shavon was returned to the same hospital room and was face down on the bed again. This time, with both cheeks being treated, no one even bothered to cover her bare butt.

"Thank you. But you said it was the fault of one of the Detectives that you got shot."

"Well, it was Detective Lavon Tyler's fault. See, he had me dressed in a clown costume. Well, I couldn't run. Thank God for the rough-looking lady cop. Was so quick on the draw."

Wendell decided to mine the confusing statements of Shavon a little longer, then decided he would go back and check in on Webber. The doctors would most likely be finished with her shoulder. As Wendell walked the corridor toward the recovery rooms, he noticed a man trying not to remain inconspicuous. Wendell realized who the man was.

"Police freeze," Wendell yelled.

The man turned toward Wendell and reached inside his jacket. Wendell shot him in the knee, and the man dropped to the floor. Wendell pointed the gun at the man's face. "You are the Sheriff of

Nottingham, but what is more important, one of your friends put a bullet in one of my best friends. Give me a reason not to shoot you right here and now."

"Look, no need to do that. I give up. I think we can make a deal. I made a deal with Robin Hood, and he can pull money out of thin air. We could both be millionaires."

Lavon had the cold phone line routed to Nash's office. Lavon sat with Nash, Lopez, and Abby ready to take the call on speaker from Robin Hood.

"Good evening, Robin."

"Well, you must be Sir Lavon. Sir Lavon, are you still wearing that hideous Chesterfield jacket."

"No, they had a sale on tweed. What can I do for you?"

"Well, I see; as the leader of the pack that hounds us, I find you and your associate policemen much better a challenge than the Sheriff of Nottingham."

"Thank you, I think."

"Stand down and give me and my merry men safe passage for twenty-four hours, and I will not only give you the Sheriff of Nottingham, but I will not pillage your meager police computer system."

"Well, that sounds fair to me, but you have to give me a few minutes to decide. See, you have a few men, Harper, Little John, Friar Tuck, and Archer, to confer with. I must be sure I got the attention of a couple hundred people."

"Abby smiled, as did Lopez; they knew Lavon had made progress in figuring out what was happening. They themselves knew there was something not quite right about the request of Robin Hood. The clerk rushed into the room and handed a note marked urgent to Lavon. Lavon smiled. "I was sorry to hear about Maid Marian."

"Yes, when we regroup, I will select another. What do you say I will contact you back in an hour for your decision. Surely a man who returned a king's ransom can come to a decision in that time." And Robin Hood asked Norman Feinberg to hang up.

The small group in Nash's new office sat staring at each other. Finally, Lopez spoke. "How many ways was that call wrong?"

"I think the guy is deranged," Nash observed.

"Not at all. They use these false identities like a mask to hide their high intellect. They probably rehearse and have meeting testing each other, making sure no one slips up and reveals what a threat they really are."

"One thing for sure, he isn't in our computer system," Lopez stated. "No paperwork shows you or Abby having anything to do with this case. He picked you some other way."

"Look, I got to alert the Chief of Police and the Mayor before the shit hits the fan any worse than it has. It will be their decision." Nash said in a commanding voice.

"No, that's what they want. I just figured out most of it. The note I got was from Wendell. He bagged the sheriff of Nottingham less than an hour ago." Eyes around the room popped. "If he were in or system, he would know that. He isn't in our system not because he can't get in. Its because he shut his system down to move it." Lavon explained.

"That's why he wanted to be able to clog traffic so in an hour or two, when we figure out he is playing us, our pursuit would look like a herd of turtles."

"So where is he, Lavon?" Lopez asked.

"I don't know, but I know someone who does, and I give you a hint. He had the cold phone number. Who do we know that is slutty enough to sweet talk some dumb and unsuspecting cop out of the cold phone number?" Lavon riddled.

"Alright, guys, it's time we go yank the puta's hair out by the roots," Lopez commented.

"Gee, Detective Lopez, I never knew you spoke Spanish." Nash joked. Nash and Lopez had worked as partners in the past.

"Only on special occasions."

Chapter 17

Lavon knew the best way to find Vinita Gonzalez, the newswoman was by finding the camera truck assigned to her. He put out a radio call for anyone spotting news vans to contact the switchboard. He and Abby then made a map showing where Vinta usual news van had been spotted. Lavon then played a hunch. To move two mini mainframes, the cooling until and all the computer hardware, the merry men were moving had to take a truck. They called the local truck rental and scored a jackpot with the first call. The name was false for the credit card, this told them they were on the right track. Someone had anonymously rented a moving truck, and the address was local.

"So, what's the plan?" Nash asked, leaning over Abby's shoulder as they all surveyed the map.

"I say we use their plan against them. We send out uniform cops to all the local intersections. We manually turn the stop signs off and hand directs the traffic."

"Brilliant," Lopez shouted. "We box their ass in without them knowing it's our traffic jam, not theirs."

"Then we walk right up and say hello," Lavon added.

"I say once we see Vinita, we take her into protective custody. There is a dangerous felon in the area. And we are about to make an arrest." Lopez smirked. "Of course, it will be sad if she misses the story altogether."

"HOW'S MY MAKEUP. IT won't be long." Vinita asked the cameraman. Before he could answer Lavon, Lopez, and Abby stepped from behind the news van with two uniformed officers. "Look, Tyler if we are going to do a threesome, the way it works is it's you, me, and one other girl," Vinita said, staring at Lopez and Abby. "If we are doing a foursome, that mean you bring one other girl and an extra dick. So, unless Blackwell is packing a nine."

"Please, Lavon don't do this to me. He promised me an exclusive interview on how he outwitted the police." Vinita cried out as the officers led her and the cameraman away.

"You can't arrest me. I am a journalist on a story."

"That's why you aren't being arrested, you Puta Pintada. You are being put into protective custody until we make an arrest." Lopez explained.

"SO, WHAT DID YOU HAVE to give that slut from the news to get the name of the cop in charge and a number to reach him?" Friar Tuck, Chandler Redgren asked.

The group sat stalled in a large, rented truck full of computer equipment, games, and personal possessions. The traffic inched forward and then stopped repeatedly.

"We could have loaded this shit in will barrels and rolled it down the street by no." Harper, Joshua Franklin complained, reaching his boiling point.

Robin, Norton Feinberg, Harper, and Tuck sat crammed in the truck's front cab. Little John and Archer, Millard Hoffland rode in back with the load.

It did not take long to find the truck with the merry men. It was stuck in traffic. Lavon walked casually up from behind the truck a stuck his gun in Norton's ear. "Might I suggest you keep your hands on the wheel. You would be surprised what a mess this gun can cause at this distance." Abby appeared at the opposite side of the trunk and prompted the passengers to comply. Sargent Rush and a group of uniformed officers surprised the passengers in the back of the truck, and Robin Hood and his merry men were apprehended.

"How could you low IQ morons find us?" Norton complained.

"The king's ransom you mentioned was the Appleton Treasure. I was wearing the Chesterfield jacket when I was interviewed by Vinita. Due to some stains Abby put on the jacket, I burned it after that night. But it did tell me who you would have talked to and got the cold phone number from." Lavon smiled at Norton's discomfort in making a simple mistake." So that told me who you talked to, the one person that insists that I am lead on a case whether or not it's true."

Chapter 18

"I don't understand why anyone wears these things anyway," Webber complained as Shelia, her wife helped her tie her bow tie. Webber had left the hospital just in time to attend the Police vs Fireman's boxing match. Both Lavon and Wendell won easily, winning their weight classes. Now Webber was preparing to be the best person for Wendell's wedding. Webber still had her arm in a sling, which meant there was no way for her to tie the tie herself.

"Don't just watch me help," Shelia instructed Lavon. Lavon and Shelia had only met two nights before at the boxing match.

"I hear you were the second choice for the best man." Shelia prodded Lavon.

"It's best person, and she is the best person."

"I guess I feel a little jealous of the two of them having such a tight friendship with none of the prejudices of mankind to block it. Not fueled by physical love or bound by a contract. Now if you guys would just stop getting her shot at."

The wedding was far grander and better attended than Nya or Wendell would have imagined. The Shepherds Pass General Hospital crowed strongly supported Nya working for the hospital. What looked like the entire fire department was in attendance since Wendell had defeated their light heavyweight champ in the charity boxing event and since Webber is married to one of their own. And the Shepherd Pass Police force made a strong showing—Webber and been given a medal of bravery and a citation for courage under direct fire. The mayor attended.

At the end of the wedding, Lynn caught the bouquet. The happy couple ran up to Lavon and Lynn and thanked them for their gift and were off to the reception.

"I got them a baby Bassett, and I put both our names on it," Lavon whispered to Lynn when Wendell and Nya were out of hearing range.

"I know that's why I gave them two weeks in Hawaii all-inclusive and put our names on it. What kind of person gives baby gifts for a wedding present." She thought for a moment. "Forget that considering the size of your family, you people probably have to give baby gifts at Halloween."

Abby chose not to attend the wedding; instead, she lent appropriate clothes to Shavon and drove her to the train station to be sure she left Shepherds Pass, clearly not caring where Shavon went as long as it was far away from Shepherds Pass.

Just as it has been the duty of lighthouses for hundreds of years to guide ships safely into harbors. Thank you for allowing us at the Looking Glass Lighthouse to steer your thoughts dreams and imagination safely to a port of enjoyment.

We are pleased that you have chosen to join us on this journey.

Please feel free to send feedback, questions, and comments to Lookingglasslighthouse@gmail.com and be sure to make your preferred literature vendor aware of your experience.

AS A SPECIAL THANK you for allowing us to entertain you we would like to give you a special sneak peek into a due to be released soon work by Alex Mitchell. Man Among the Missing

Chapter One

M osses rushed into the Eastern Star Cleaners.

Marta was business waiting on an elderly lady that seemed confused about her change.

"Yes, ma'am, this is the correct amount."

"I guess I must have thought it cost less. Did you raise your prices?" The old woman asked in an accusatory tone.

Mosses looked shaken, and it was clear to Marta that he wanted to talk to her. Jacob, the other person that worked with them at the cleaners, noticed the agitation in Mosses and grew nervous. Mosses did much of the pressing in the shop and seemed never to look up from his work in customers were in the store.

"No, ma'am, we have not raised any prices in over two years.

All our customers would go to the larger cleaner if we did."

The old woman gathered her goods and gave a slight smile as if that was the answer she wanted to hear.

"You have got to contact the handler and pull the plug on this operation." Mosses pleaded as the three gathered in the small office in the rear of the cleaners.

"Has our cover been blown? What did you learn at the mosque today?" Jacob asked, dropping the fake middle eastern accent he used for his cover.

"No, my cover was not blown. In fact, I now know where the bank we are looking for is located.

The man I have been shadowing was there today, and I have his trust." Mosses swallowed and gasped like he was having trouble breathing. There was clearly more to be said, but the rush of information was overwhelming.

"Then this is good news." Marta defined.

"Not at all. The reason he trusts me is that they have been following us, and they believe we are genuine terrorists because the is a federal team watching us too.

"Protection?" Marta hypothesized.

"He says they look like an extraction team. He has seen plenty in the middle east. Most likely private contractors."

"Limited private contractors are operating on US soil." Jacob looked confused.

The chime of the little bell over the door alerting to the entry of a customer sounded, and the three came forward.

"We give a discount to first responders," Marta called out as she led the trio out of the small office. Her offer came with her straining to speak understandable English. There were four people dressed in city police uniforms standing facing the counter. As a trained agent, she knew there was something wrong. Live through this encounter, Marta thought. Don't break the cover. Marta began to assess. They were not just standing randomly. They were covering the room. Some sort of tactical formation. The look on their faces was focused; they were ready for a rough encounter. And even though their uniforms and badges said ST. Louis City Police, they were carrying the wrong type of weapons.

"We did not come to get our clothes pressed. We had a few questions." The tall, strong-looking man in his forties spoke. He had a pockmarked face and a steely gaze like he was reading a map that was sitting too far away.

There were two other male officers and two female officers in the cleaners. An additional male officer could be seen through the storefront window guarding the entrance to the cleaners. A stocky pale-skinned female officer with a red buzz cut started to walk behind the counter, and Moses blocked her.

"Step aside, Sambo," Red commanded.

Mosses stood there staring straight ahead and not moving. He had endured many racial insults in the military academy and knew them for what they were.

"Relax, Mosses, we have nothing to hide," Jacob called to Mosses.

"That's right Nigger Jim, be a good nigger and step aside, and while you are at it, show me some ID. And it had better not be your grandmother's food stamp card."

"It is not necessary to insult him," Jacob shouted from the back of the room.

"I tell you what, why do you all pony up some current valid ID." The officer in charge commanded.

Red and Mosses still seemed locked in, staring at each other. Red made a half turn to fake, then spun around to punch Mosses in the face.

Mosses had boxed golden gloves before being accepted at West Point. Mosses slipped her punch and let the force from the would-be blow cause her to fall off balance and almost hit the floor. The other officers found this entertaining. Red did not. Red raced toward Mosses to grab him and wrestle him, but he held up the heel of his hand, and it hit her like the force of running full speed into a wall. She dropped to her knees.

"Stop this shit. The kid is clearly not trained to stand still and take a beating. No peaceful protesting or singing we shall overcome while you beat the shit out of him.' The commander praised the skill level of Mosses. Moses leaned forward to help the female officer up; the universal no harm intended move. She lay half kneeling and nursing a nosebleed. Then something Mosses had never experienced overtook him. The light in the room seemed to dim, and a rush of air seemed to pass his ears. For a moment, he could swear he heard the voice of his late grandmother singing one of the old negro spirituals she used to sign on her way to church in Georgia. Mosses looked over at Marta and could not identify the look on her face, but she was staring at him. His midsection to be more precise. It hurt. He looked down at his midsection, and there was Red's hand. She had something in it. It was the handle of a knife, and the blade was buried deep within his stomach.

Mosses was sad not that he knew he was dying but that he had let Marta and Jacob down. He was the youngest of the team, and his inexperience was marring the operation. There was screaming from behind him. Then the screaming stopped at the end of automatic gunfire. It was Jacob that had been silenced.

"Bag the bodies if there is a bounty on either of them, I want us to get it. Bag the chick." The commander ordered. "And call the translator team that was recommended let's see what this one has to say."

Marta felt the nylon tie bind her from the back as a dark see through hood was placed over her head. She felt an over personal and over aggressive searching of her person and one last statement rang in her ears. It was from the commander. "Alright boys and girls let's get the fuck out of her before the real cops show up."

"SO. THIS IS THE PART where I fold the whipped egg whites into the batter." Alexis stated to Vincent Garrison. Vincent felt proud that his daughter Lisa and his next-door neighbor's daughter Alexis love to get cooking lessons from him. He also tutored them both in math even though Lisa, being eighteen and preparing for college, was at a higher level than Alexis.

"Now the trick is to wait until the oil is just the right temperature before adding the batter. Corn oil works best for pancakes and canola if you don't have it but never use a meat rendering.

The smoke point is too low. It will burn your product and taste burned."

"Oh my God what are you doing." Lowell Waterman entered the room from the kitchen. The Waterman's are Vincent Garrisons neighbors. The Garrison back door has a keypad lock and Vincent insisted that all the Waterman's know the combination. Lowell entered with his nine-year-old son Donny.

"Cornflakes," Donny screamed, and the small copper-colored puppy named Cornflakes rushed out to greet his favorite playmate.

"Mr. Garrison is teaching me to make Mississippi Pecan Pancakes."

"Not that. Where is your robe?" Lowell scolded.

"Well, I was cooking, and it was warm. Besides, Mr. Garrison doesn't see me that way." She turned to Vincent. "Do you." Alexis stood wearing a nightshirt that was probably the perfect size two years ago but now looked like she was blossoming in all the right places.

Vincent walked over to where Alexis had left the robe and handed it to her. "It is not about how I look at you. It is about your father asking you to do something and you questioning it. Do what he asks first. Then ask your question. The time we fathers have with our daughters goes so fast it need not be marred with defiance."

"God, I am sorry, Daddy. Sit, and you can be my first customer."

Lowell shot Vincent a look of gratitude for the parental backup.

"Oh my," Lowell exclaimed as he tasted the pancakes. "Why aren't you teaching my wife to cook."

"Because she is hopeless," Alexis mumbled.

"I heard that." Sharon Waterman explained, appearing from the kitchen in search of her missing family. "You are a traitor, Lowell Waterman. I send you to retrieve my children, and I find you eating pancakes."

"It was my duty as a parent to check her culinary progress. And my God, are there good."

"Sit mom, you get the next batch."

"Mr. Garrison, Cornflakes says he wants to go outside to do his business," Donny called over the other conversation.

"Then, by all means take him outside, and maybe someday you can let me in on how the two of you talk to each other. It could save me countless carpet cleanings."

This brought a round of laughs from the group.

"Will Lisa be back soon?" Susan Waterman asked Vincent with a note of concern ringing in her voice.

"She is visiting her mom in Chicago. She should be back tomorrow. I keep thinking she will be off to college soon, and my nest will be empty." Vincent may have started the statement to be glib, but his eyes gave him away.

Don't miss out!

Visit the website below and you can sign up to receive emails whenever Alex Mitchell publishes a new book. There's no charge and no obligation.

https://books2read.com/r/B-A-UGUAB-GFXOC

BOOKS 2 READ

Connecting independent readers to independent writers.

Also by Alex Mitchell